DRAGON SCALE

A GUIDE TO DRAGONS

(from smallest to largest)

by Jessica Cathryn Feinberg

Special Thanks to:

The AMAZING Kickstarter backers
who funded this project!

Alese, Cary, John, and the gang
at Epic Cafe for their friendship,
feedback and support throughout
the creation of this book!

My amazing supportive
facebook fans and friends!

Victoria Morris for
her support, feedback,
and awesome editing skills!

SECOND EDITION APRIL 2014

Where are the dragons?

Dragons are alive and well in the world around us at this very moment.

Why don't more people see them? There are many reasons. The surviving species of dragons have mastered the art of going unnoticed. Some have the ability to move too fast for us to easily spot. Others can blend in so well with their environment that we mistake them for rocks, trees, and even other animals.

The hardest to spot of the dragons are those that seem to have the ability to simply not be noticed no matter how big or crazy they may look. Most people can look right at them, yet not notice them.

There are many theories as to why this is. The most accepted is that our modern world denies their existence to such an extent that people simply cannot accept dragons as a part of their reality. For these people dragons simply do not exist so they cannot see them.

This book was created to give the reader a view into the world of dragons, and, for those who wish to observe dragons, serve as a field guide.

6 Dragon Spotting Tips:

1. Learn to sit very still and be patient.

2. Always be on the lookout, especially from the corner of your eye - dragons are really stealthy.

3. Look for signs of a dragon's presence. (see specific dragons for details)

4. Use bait if needed. (see specific dragons for details)

5. Allow dragons to exist for you. Let them be a part of your world and your reality.

6. Remember: If you don't believe you will see one, you probably never will.

Dragon Types

There many different definitions for dragon "types". This book uses the "types" defined below. Note that dragons can be more than one type. Dragons in this book are organized smallest to largest, but you can look them up alphabetically or by type using the indexes at the back of the book.

Western Dragons are the best known dragons and generally have reptilian features and 2-4 limbs. They may or may not have wings.

Western

Drakes are usually a subset of western dragons that tend to be a little smaller and either have no wings, or their wings are smaller and cannot carry them very far.

Eastern

Eastern Dragons usually have more dog-like features and may have fur or whiskers. They are usually long, skinny dragons with 2 to 8 limbs and may or may not have wings.

Wyrms are dragons without limbs or wings.

Aquatic Hydra

Wyverns are winged dragons that have up to two limbs (they may not have any).

Hydras are dragons with multiple heads.

Avian

Aquatic Dragons are dragons that dwell in water and generally have some fish like features (like fins).

Avian Dragons are dragons with bird like features such as beaks, talons, and feathers.

Insectoid

Insectoid Dragons are dragons with insect like features such as extra jointed limbs, and wings that resemble butterflies or dragonflies.

Clockwork Dragons are made of metal and gears. Usually a type of machine inhabited by a dragon spirit.

Clockwork

Actual size →

Magnification

Nano Drake
Parva metallum draconis

One of the smallest dragons known to exist, the Nano Drake is only 1/10th of an inch (or sometimes smaller!) in size! This clockwork dragon is said to have been engineered to make tiny repairs that human hands would be too clumsy for. Unfortunately, something went wrong with the design and the drakes became destructive. Most unexplained small holes in clothing, rust spots, bug bites, and other mysterious damage can be traced back to this malicious creature. Nano drakes usually travel in groups.

Common Thread Nibbler
Orientales filo comedenti

A small (2-3 inch long) wingless dragon, usually tinted blue or green. Males tend to have brighter coloration. Frequents sewing baskets, thread factories, and giftwrap suppliers.

The Thread Nibbler cannot resist pulling, chewing, biting, and knotting threads, strings and cords.

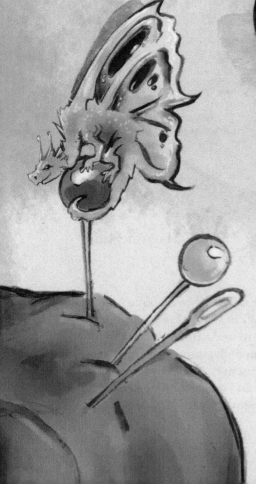

Pin Flicker
Veloces latro acus

A tiny (1/8 to 1/4 inch) yellow-orange hued dragon with antennae and dark spotted patterning. The Pin Flicker moves at an incredibly swift speed. They are extremely rare to spot and are known for rearranging pins, needles and other sharp objects in the blink of an eye.

Most often inhabits small sewing basketsand forgotten desk drawers.

Pencil Percher
Penicillo perticatam

This tiny (1/4-1/2 inch) dragon is often
found perched on small objects.
The Pencil Percher enjoys digging its
claws into erasers and is usually nocturnal.
Attracted to bright colors, these dragons
are often midnight muses for artists.

Lucky Chomper
Felix rememorando secum

Another tiny (1-2 inch) dragon, the Chomper lives in
a constant state of teething and derives his name from
commonly chewing on six sided dice. Urban myths say
dice with tiny chomper marks are usually lucky, but there
has never been scientific proof of this.

Golden Tipped
Leaf Drake

Yellow Faced
Field Drake

Grasshopper Drakes
Cicada draconis

Some of the smallest dragons (1/2-1 inch long), grasshopper drakes derive their name from being commonly mistaken for grasshoppers. A form of insectoid dragon, these drakes have segmented carapaces and double sets of wings. Depending on the exact variety they may also have antennae or horns.

Grasshopper drakes are herbivores and feed on grasses and leaves.

Autumn Drake (in flight)

Long Tailed Apple Drake
Apple draco insidens

The apple drake is a little over 1/4 inch in size and can be found, most often, in apple orchards.

Drawn to the bright green and red apples, this drake feeds upon apple blossoms and makes a soft humming sound when flying. Often mistaken for a bee.

Golden Apple Wyrm
Aureum pomum dracone

At around an inch in length it is easy to mistake this eastern dragon for an every day worm. Its diet consists of apples and it often nests inside them. Less common than the apple drake, the apple wyrm prefers tart apples when possible.

Bluebell Draconis
Hyacinthoides draco

This small 1-2 inch dragon is commonly found
around bluebell plants. Has a very long tongue
that can snap out to catch small butterflies and
other insects. Great for pest extermination and
generally friendly.

Blue Bee Chaser
Sectator apis draco

This sky blue drake is only about 2 inches from nose to tail and is common in most gardens, especially those with any type of daisy. They are rarely spotted due to their speed and ability to blend in with the sky behind them. A playful creature, the Bee Chaser, spends its days in an endless game of tag with any nearby bumble bees. It is unknown where these creatures go during colder months, the common theory is that they hibernate near dormant bee hives.

J. FEINBERG

Teacup Drake
Camellia sinensis draco

Native to East, South and Southeast Asia, the teacup drake spread with the cultivation of tea and is now common throughout the western countries as well. This small (2 inch) drake inhabits nooks and crannies much like a mouse would, but is drawn to tea rather than cheese. Can be baited with a high quality, freshly steeped, cup of earl gray.

Fan Finned Sea Serpent
Serpentis maris segmentum

Only about 2 inches long, this fierce looking
sea monster goes unnoticed by most due to its
size. Feeds mostly on tiny fish and shrimp.
Lives in shallow tidal pools and hides in small
caves and the hollows between rocks.

Vine Drake
Vitis draco

Commonly found on vines, espeically grape vines. A herbivore,
the vine drake is around 2.8 inches and does, indeed, feed on
grapes. Uses its tail for clinging to vines while sleeping or eating.
Native to the Mediterranean and Central Asia.

Ruby Breasted Flower Drake
Rubinus avis dracone

Often mistaken for a hummingbird, this tiny (2-3 inch) drake is often found around brightly colored, sweet smelling, flowers. Like hummingbirds, flower drakes move very rapidly - flapping their wings up to 70 times each second! This species favors red flowers.

Red Rumped Nut Hoarder
Draco nucem furari

At 3 inches this dragon is often mistaken for a rodent, most commonly a chipmunk. Typically found in North America, the nut hoarder has an omnivorous diet consisting of nuts and seeds. Those in colder climates hibernate during the winter, while those in the southwest often survive off hoarded stores of nuts in their burrows. Often the prey of larger carnivores.

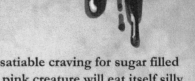

Frosting Snatcher
Gelu rapientem draco

This small (2.3 inches) dragon has an insatiable craving for sugar filled toppings. Found in many bakeries, this pink creature will eat itself silly on any accessible sweets.

Guzzler Gremlin
Lurco draco

Only slightly more dignified is the guzzler, a green dragon 2.6 inches in size. The guzzler is known for taking huge bites, and rather than leaving a mess will leave nothing behind at all - licking a plate so clean that you'd swear there was never food on it to begin with.

Sugar Wyvern
Saccharo draco

3 inches in size, this blue dragon can scent out anything with sugar, even though closed doors and sealed dishes. No treats are safe around these dragons. Best baited with colorful desserts with high sugar content.

Syrup Slurper
Sirupus sorbitio draco

This teal dragon is addicted to sugar in a more liquid form and will hunt down any type of syrup from chocolate to maple. VERY greedy and can be highly aggressive. 2.4 inches.

Cherry Chomper
Comedenti cerasorum draco

Slightly healthier, the yellow cherry chomper prefers sugar filled fruits like cherries. Bait them with candied orange slices for best results. More docile (possibly from a constant sugar coma state), they make good pets if you can catch one. 3.1 inches.

Coconut Drake
Cocos nucifera draco

This small (3 inch) drake not only feeds on coconuts, but also likes to built nests and dens from their shells. These tiny dragons have very sharp teeth capable of cracking coconut shells, which allows them to drink the milk and eventually (after some additional claw work to open it the rest of the way) eat the coconut.

These once common dragons are now rare due to pirates hunting them for their teeth in the 1700's.

Lesser Pine Drake
Pinus draco minor

Common in alpine climates, pine drakes nest inside the trunks of pine trees, the older the better. 2-3 inches. Enjoys chewing pine cones and usually feeds on pine nuts and other small seeds. Dragon watchers have had best results by baiting them with peanut butter covered pinecones hung from tree branches.

Lillypad Draconis
Nymphaeaceae draco

A small (3.2 inch) toad-like dragon, partly aquatic with
tadpole-like water dwelling young. Feeds on small insects.
Found near ponds and will emerge most during rainfall.

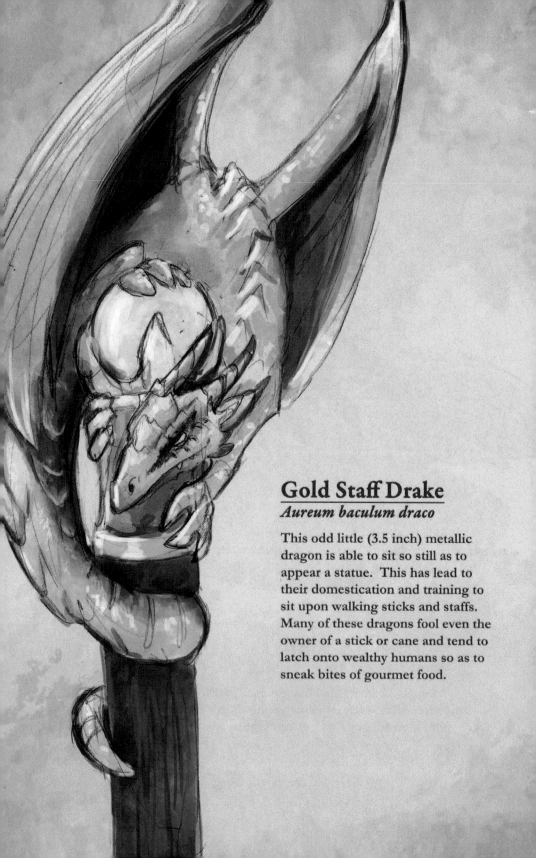

Gold Staff Drake
Aureum baculum draco

This odd little (3.5 inch) metallic dragon is able to sit so still as to appear a statue. This has lead to their domestication and training to sit upon walking sticks and staffs. Many of these dragons fool even the owner of a stick or cane and tend to latch onto wealthy humans so as to sneak bites of gourmet food.

Ice Cube Snatcher

Glacies cubum furem

This strange little dragon stands around 3.8 inches tall and is usually iridescent blue/green in color. While most hoarding dragons collect objects that last (from bottle caps to gold!), this dragon steals ice cubes. This puzzling behavior is attributed to possible Ice Drake linage which leads to an affinity for cold. It is yet unexplained why this species seems to only take ice cubs while ignoring other forms of ice and snow.

Peanut Butter Drake

Arachis hypogaea draco

Found in cupboards and supermarkets this very odd little (4.1 inch) dragon is addicted very specifically to peanut butter. It does not seem to react to regular butter or be fooled by other nut butters. Yet when peanut butter is left open one of these dragons is sure to be nearby and sure to make a mess.

Tooth Hoarder

Dentes furem draco

Around 4.2 inches in size, these dragons hoard teeth. They are non
aggressive and usually scavenge discarded teeth or those of the dead.
Oddly, they sometimes leave other small objects such as gems, coins,
or seashells in place of the teeth they collect. This is thought to be the
basis of the tooth fairy mythology.

Pearl Guardian
Custos margaritis

This small (4-6 Inch) eastern dragon usually guards a pearl. Unlike hoarding dragons, the pearl guardian will not have as many pearls as it can find. Instead it chooses just one pearl and will guard it with its life. The pearls of these dragons are said to have magical powers and bring wisdom and good luck. In addition they are usually flawless and very valuable. During the Han Dynasty these dragons were often hunted for their pearls making them much more rare to see today.

Rodent Drake
Amicus mures draco

This good natured dragon often lives with, or close to small
rodents such as mice. Often protecting the mice, this symbiotic
relationship is one of the strangest in the animal kingdom.
Around 4-5 inches. Eats seeds, berries, and small beetles.

Lesser Lather Drake
Draco de saponem

Common to bathrooms and kitchens, this small (5.8 inch) blue dragon feeds almost solely on soap. Very fast and somewhat slippery, possibly due to their strange diet, these dragons are almost impossible to catch. Lather drakes also hoard bits of soap for later consumption and are known to collect a variety. This may indicate a very discerning palate, at least where soap is concerned.

Green-Backed Shredder
Draco qui correptum

At 4.3 inches in height, this small dragon may not
seem intimidating, but the shredder can destroy
paper at an astounding rate! The shredder does
not feed on paper, rather it seems to have a
compulsion to shred it into small pieces, mostly
using its teeth.

Shredders can be found in bathrooms,
libraries, bookstores, offices and anywhere
else where paper is abundant.

Orange Gremlin
Parva draco tribulatiónibus

Known for general mischief this
dragon is a close relative of the
larger cupboard gremlin. In
addition to its color the orange
gremlin can be identified by its
blunt snout and squat four legged
posture. Adults are around
6 inches long.

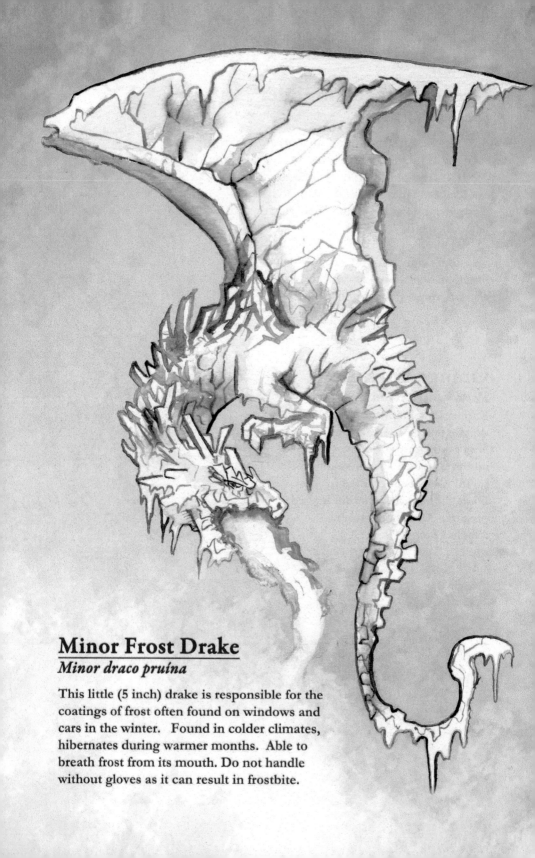

Minor Frost Drake
Minor draco pruina

This little (5 inch) drake is responsible for the coatings of frost often found on windows and cars in the winter. Found in colder climates, hibernates during warmer months. Able to breath frost from its mouth. Do not handle without gloves as it can result in frostbite.

Red-Scaled Cookie Crumbler
Crustulum furem

Unable to resist the lure of baked goods, this small (4-6 inches) dragon frequently plagues pantries, bakeries, and cookie factories. Children are often mistakenly blamed for the capers of this beast who is known to devour pasties at lightning speed. The fastest crumbler on record was able to completely ingest a 4.5 inch cookie in under two seconds. Coloration varies from red to deep purple.

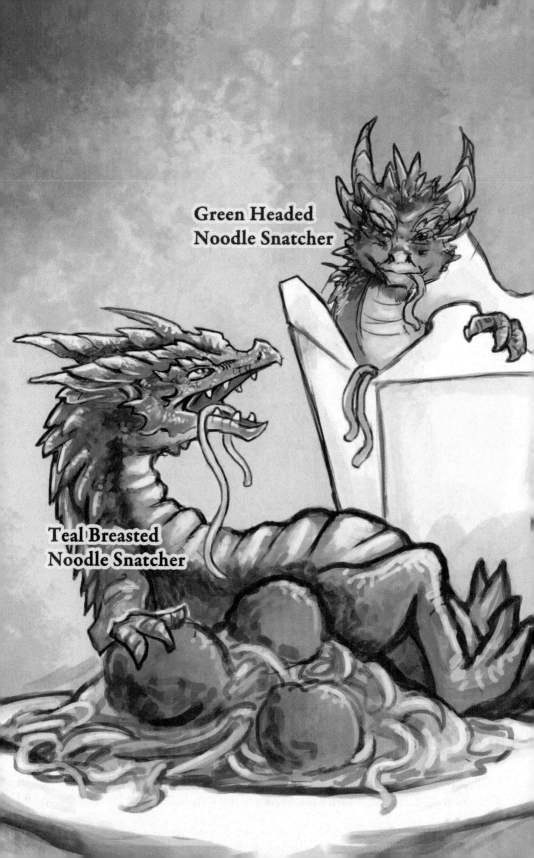

Noodle Snatcher
Draco rapientem pasta

Common in Japanese, Chinese and Italian eateries, the noodle snatcher is a small (5.4 inch) dragon who feeds primarily upon pasta. Contrary to its rather rotund appearance, this is a very fast moving dragon. Noodle snatchers have been known to devour a bowl of pasta in under sixty seconds and be out of sight again before you know it.

There are many varieties of noodle snatcher, but they can usually be identified by their pronounced ridged horns and rounded bellies.

Purple Crested Noodle Snatcher

Bakery Drake
Pistrinum habitaculum draco

This little (5.3 inch) brightly colored eastern
dragon is the best kept secret of many bakeries.
Oddly, this dragon enjoys assisting with
kneading of dough and its delicate touch is the
secret behind many perfect breads and pastries.

Snowdrop Drake
Galanthus draco

Most common in the early spring months, snowdrop drakes are usually hidden under thick beds of flowers and can only be spotted by the most patient of dragon watchers. Their coloration is a deep green with a milky white belly. Some snowdrop drakes have touches of deeper orange colors. Approximately 5.9 inches from nose to tail.

Ink Gremlin
Draco de atramento vertuntur

Around 5 inches, the ink gremlin is known
for swiftly knocking over bottles of ink.
It is unclear where this instinct to spill
comes from, but this dragon is so fast
that its presence is only detectable
by the inky footprints left in its wake.

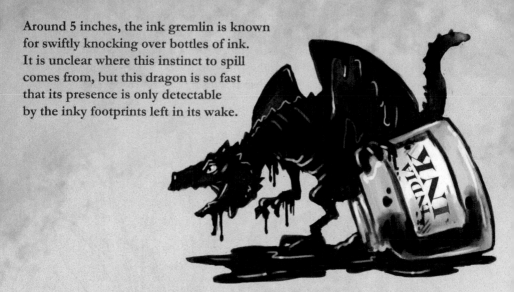

Paper Gremlin
Draco qui furatur libellis

This small (8 inch) red dragon may look
harmless, but it is often to blame when
papers go missing.

From to-do lists to homework to
contracts, the paper gremlin is
adept at spiriting away documents
just when you need them most!

Toadstool Drake
Draco fungos

Living in and feeding on mushrooms of all sizes, this 6 inch dragon inhabits forests and small caverns. While immune to poisonous mushrooms, some varieties can cause the toadstool drake to hallucinate causing erratic and jittery behavior.

Household Chameleon
Draconem in aperto

This odd little (6 inch) dragon is very common around most households, but very hard to spot. Chameleon dragons have the ability to change the colors of their scales to blend in perfectly wherever they are. Usually these are very docile and even caring creatures, depending on the given household.

Minor Water Dragon
Minima aqueous draconis

One of the smallest (6 inches) water dragons, it is
often mistaken for seaweed due to its flowing fins.
A herbivore, the minor water dragon is tame enough
to co-habit with other fish and makes an excellent
addition to any aquarium, provided you can catch one.

Wire Nibbler
Exterminatore filum his

Commonly sneaks under and behind desks. Coloration a deep metallic purple. Cannot resist chewing on cables and wires. Seems immune to electric shock. Usually around 7 inches. Able to destroy a power cord in 4 minutes flat. Spay cables with hot pepper to deter them.

Cupboard Gremlin
Armarium malum draco

This small (around 7 inch) dragon loves to lurk in dark cupboards and pantries. Usually green in color, the "gremlin" has a serious sweet tooth and cannot resist the lure of frosting. Rarely caught, this stealthy dragon is responsible for the destruction of countless cupcakes, eclairs, and layer cakes.

Common Grass Drake
Draco herba

This small (7 inch), odd looking dragon, is a distant cousin of the moss dragon. The grass drake takes his name from the grass like spines on its back and the fact that it encourages the growth of actual grass and other plant life there.

This allows the dragon to flop onto it's stomach and blend in with the ground, appearing to be nothing more than a lump in the grass.

Blue Grass Drake
Draco herba caeruleo

Slighting larger than the common variety, the blue grass drake is around 8-9 inches and, of course, much more blue in color. This dragon is more rare to spot and lurks around blue colored grasses, usually the varieties considered ornamental by gardeners such as Festuca cinerea and Koeleria glauca.

Blue Banded Pen Snatcher
Calamum rapientem

Best identified by the blue banding on its back, this small (7.8 inches from nose to tail) dragon suffers from a compulsive need to take pens. Oddly, this nocturnal dragon seems to ignore other types of writing implements and only snatches pens.

Studies show that the pen snatcher has some sort of instinctive sense that enables it to tell how much ink remains in a given pen. They always favor pens with more ink, over those that have run out.

Malicious Literary Drake

Malum librum perditoris

8 inches of devious malevolence, this drake takes great pleasure in
ripping key pages from books to the frustration of readers everywhere.
Commonly found in the dusty back corners of libraries and bookstores.
Usually purple or black in coloration.

Stamp Snatcher
Consumens resinae draco

This dragon is addicted to licking the coating found on postage stamps and stickers and steals them as often as possible. 8.5 inches. Aggressive when frightened.

Coffee Drake
Capulus dracone

The coffee drake is aptly named for its addiction to coffee.
While the smell of any coffee will lure this beast,
caffeinated, strong, high quality blends
work best. Measures 8-9 inches long.
Non-aggressive, but it is not wise
to come between this drake
and a cup of coffee.

Rose Wyrm
Rosa serpens draco

Vaguely resembling a cobra, adult rose wyrms are 8 to 10 inches in length and are usually found near rosebushes. Like the cobra, these wyrms have a neurotoxic venom that can be deadly, so one should approach them warily. Their hardened outer scales render them immune to rose thorns.

Mold Drake
Draco fingunt

Common in abandoned houses, behind washing machines and under sinks. This small (8 inch) dragon has the ability to breath mold. Mold drakes should generally be avoided. When one must be approached protective gear is suggested.

Key Snatcher
Rapientem instrumentum clavem

This small (9 inch) dragon steals the keys from keyboards of all kinds including computer and piano keyboards. They prefer to snatch more unusual letter keys such as "X" and "Z", possibly because they have less wear on them, but they will settle for any key in a pinch. Commonly found in junk yards and used electronics stores.

Sword Drake
Gladiis custodes draco

Historically, sword drakes guard weapons of particular significance, though they are rarely seen today. 8 to 12 inches, dwelling mostly in forgotten treasure hoards. Once this drake has selected a sword they are bonded for life and have an instinctual sense of their sword's location.

Dagger Wyrm
Custodes pugiones draco

Similar to the sword drake, this
wyrm tends to attach itself to
guarding smaller daggers. A bit
smaller (6-10 inches), these wyrms
are sometimes venomous and
able to paralyze those who try to
lay claim to their daggers.

Three Headed Hatra
Proni hydra

The hatra is a type of hydra that always has three heads and nests inside hats. Hatra can grow to be anywhere from 7 to 12 inches in length, yet are surprisingly adept at compressing themselves to fit, unnoticed, inside most hats. This type of hydra usually has iridescent coloring in blues and greens with hints of warmer colors. Hatras are known to favor stetsons and fedoras for their nests.

Utensil Hoarder
Fur utensile draco

While some dragons choose to hoard coins or gems, this odd gremlin like dragon is drawn to utensils such as forks, knives and spoons. Favoring sterling silver when available, it tends to snatch just one or two of a set leaving the set's owner somewhat baffled. Around 9 inches in size.

Common Cactus Drake

Cactaceae draco

One of the most common desert dragons, the common cactus drake ranges from 9 to 15 inches and has a variety of color variations.

Feeding mostly on insects and small lizards they can be quite territorial and usually nest within a given cacti for many years.

This dragon can breath fire in short, controlled bursts.

Yellow Cactus Drake

Blue
Cactus
Drake

Spiked Snatcher
Rapientem draco de spicis

Common to movie theaters and fast food joints, the spiked snatcher is easily distinguished from other small (10 inch) dragons by its three eyes and spiky, quill crest. Diet consists mainly of crunchy, man made foods. Unable to resist popcorn.

Citrus Drake
Rutaceae draco

Common in citrus trees/shrubs including orange, lemon, and grapefruit trees. This small (10.2 inch) dragon sports a green coloration that blends in easily with citrus trees. Citrus drakes crave vitamine C (found in most citrus fruits) and have an excellent sense of smell. They hibernate during the colder months.

Egg Snatchers
Fraudator Ovum

One of the more vicious hoarding dragons, the egg snatchers
come in a few varieties and like to steal the eggs of other animals.
They have even been known to steal the eggs of other dragons.
They eat the contents, but keep the shells as intact as possible
and line their lairs with them. Most attracted to brightly colored
or patterned eggs.

**Orange Crested
Egg Snatcher
11 inches**

Common Egg
Snatcher
9 inches

Sink Drake
Draco faucet

This iridescent drake enjoys perching on sink faucets and splashing the water as it comes out. Approximately 11 inches.

Sink Serpent
Serpens lava pelvim

Also iridescent, the sink serpent is related to larger sea serpents, but prefers to swim in small domestic water basins such as sinks and bathtubs. They can be lured with lavender scented soaps and bubble bath. Approximately 13 inches long.

Paint Drake
Pingunt furem tubus

Drawn to brightly colored paint this dragon mostly snatches paint tubes, but will also knock over cans and paint palettes. Very fast and difficult to spot, but evidence of them can be found in the form of footprints in the paint. 11 inches tall.

Grave Crawlers
De cippo draco

Grave crawlers are small (12 inch) winged drakes that
dwell in cemeteries Only active at night, these dragons
have dark and light (albino) color variations. Grave
crawlers often eat the flowers placed on graves and are
thought to bring bad luck to mourners.

Striped Candy Wyrm
Dulce virgatis furem

Smaller than the candy snatcher, the candy wyrm is only about a foot long. Identifying markers include a striped pattern along its body and ridged horns. Not surprisingly, this dragon craves anything sweet and brightly colored. This dragon is also an excellent swimmer and can sometimes be found in the vats of soda factories.

Red Eyed Key Snatcher
Fraudator claves

A small (13 inch) dragon with black or gray coloration and distinctive red eyes, the key snatcher is drawn to keys including car, house, and even bathroom keys. Hoards the keys in nests where it keeps them polished to a bright shine. Shows a disposition to metal keys over those made of other materials.

Vineyard Drake
Draco a vino

This 12-16 Inch drake can be found around vineyards and wineries. Can be baited with an expensive bottle of wine. Possibly related to the cork hoarder. Generally prefers red wines.

DRACO

CABERNET

1981

Lesser Green Library Drake
Bibliomanias draconis

A small to medium sized (13-18 inches) indoor dragon native to libraries and antiquarian booksellers. The green/yellow variant shown here is found to be partial to mystery novels. Those who wish to observe the beast will find best results baiting them with vintage first editions of Sherlock Holmes.

Blue Tome Guardian
Libro antiquo draco

Like the gold tome dragon, this smaller 13 inch blue variation also watches over rare books. However, this literary dragon chooses to watch over cook books specifically. Taking its guarding duty very seriously, it will only surrender the best of recipes to those who have proven themselves worthy by providing top quality bonbons.

Card Snatcher

Ludens pecto furem

Oddly drawn to playing cards (perhaps to do with their shape, coating or colors?), this dragon builds its nest from somewhat-chewed cards. Stealing a few from a deck, this snatcher is very fast and rarely spotted. Around 13 inches in size.

Seahorse Drake

Hippocampus draco

Up to 14 inches in size, the seahorse drake greatly resembles seahorses, but swim considerably better. With excellent camouflage they are known to ambush their prey. Usually feeds on smaller sea life. Carnivorous.

Candle Drake
Lucernam draconis

Candle drakes range from
12 to 16 inches in size and
are usually red or purple in
color. They are drawn to
candles and, depending on the
drake, can be peaceful or total
pyromaniacs. If an infestation of
candle drakes is suspected it is
advised to keep water near any
candles as they may suddenly
light themselves.

Lavatory Hydra
Latrinum Draco

The lavatory hydra, commonly known as the "Loo Snake", can grow up to 15 inches and have as many as seven heads. The smaller cousin of the sewer wyrm, this iridescent aquatic dragon has the ability to compress itself to fit though pipes and can startle the occupants of both private and public restrooms alike. Most common in the United Kingdom.

Bottlecap Hoarder
Fur uter opercula

A fan of human culture, this dragon is drawn to the shiny
nature and shape of metal bottle caps. Most favor those from
soda and beer bottles in bright colors. Hoards the caps into
large piles forming a nest upon which it sleeps. 14 inches.

Tiger-Striped Skull Snatcher
Calvariam rapientem

Skull snatchers obsessively hoard bones, usually skulls.
The tiger-striped variety favors human and primate skulls,
creating nests inside large collected piles of them.
They average about 14 inches in length.

Skull snatchers are not very
aggressive - scavenging to find
skulls of those already dead,
and seem to covet older
skulls the most.

Purple Flecked Skull Snatcher
Calvariam rapientem

A slightly larger (16 inch) and more aggressive breed of skull snatcher, this species is identified by its mottled purple markings.

Larger hoarders tend to hoard the skulls of larger animals such as horses, cattle, and dinosaurs.

Fluorescent Skull Snatcher
Calvariam rapientem

This variety of skull snatcher is distinguished by its bright florescent coloring in shades of yellow or green. Easier to spot in dark caves due it its distinctive fluorescence. More skittish and light sensitive than other varieties.

Red Ridged Skull Snatcher
Calvariam rapientem

The red ridged variety is more common in dry, desert climates.
Most aggressive of the skull snatchers, this dragon is very territorial
around its skull hoard. Diet consists of insects and small rodents.

Yellow Bellied Lace Gnawer
Bentes de corigiam

Household pets are often mistakenly blamed for the
damage caused by this wingless dragon. Averaging 1.3 feet,
the lace gnawer is easily identifiable by its green back quills
and yellow belly. A distant cousin of the thread and wire
nibblers, this dragon is known to chew the ends off shoe
laces. Prefers white laces, especially those found in shoes of
a primary color (yellow, red, or blue). When bating a trap
for the lace gnawer use shoes with longer laces such as high
tops or boots for best results.

Static Drake
Draco electrica haerent

This quirky 15 inch eastern dragon somehow manages to contain a static electric charge at all times and seems to enjoy spreading it to others. You will probably never spot a static drake without special equipment as they are very fast moving. You can, however, spot signs of them – usually these are static electric shocks or static cling without a noticeable explanation.

Cork Hoarder
Fur vini opercula

A distant relative of the bottlecap hoarder, this slightly larger (16 inch) drake hoards corks. Most drawn to wine bottle corks, possibly due to their residual odor. Dwells mostly along the California coast.

Gold Tome Guardian
Draco qui custodit libros

A cousin to the library drake this small (16 inch) golden dragon is only found around extremely rare books, usually those with information that could be dangerous if used improperly. Tome guardians are known to fiercely guard their books and only let people read them who can answer a series of brain-twisting riddles.

Long-Tailed Pepper Drake
Calidum piperis draco

Long tailed pepper drakes are about 17 inches long (including their tails) and come in two colors: blue and green. The blue variety tends to be around more mild pepper plants, is more common and more domesticated. The green variety has a fierce streak and feeds upon the hottest of peppers. While its bite is not deadly, it can be very painful, due to the hot pepper diet.

Yellow Crested Hitcher
Draco qui mutuatur equitat

At around 17 inches, this dragon has developed the strange habit of joyriding by clinging to the roof of cars on country roads. When noticed this can cause accidents, but usually the hitcher ditches the car when it hears another approaching.

Pumpkin Hydra
Multis capitibus draconis cucurbita

Most commonly found in pumpkin patches in October, the Pumpkin Hydra is a small (1.3 foot) multi headed dragon. This peculiar dragon hollows out pumpkins (and other gourds) to nest inside. Many believe our modern day jack-o'-lanterns were first inspired by pumpkin hydra nests. Usually avoiding human contact, this hydra is only aggressive when it feels its pumpkin is threatened. Number of heads ranges from three to five.

Knot Gremlins
Factorem malum implexi

Around 18 inches, the knot gremlins come in a variety of colors, but all suffer from an irresistible impulse to tie knots in things. They are very VERY fast at this – able to knot a cord in the blink of an eye.

While they are almost impossible to catch in the act, any mysterious tangled or knotted cords are usually a sign they are around. More so if you cannot figure out how the knots would have occurred. Their favorite things to knot are the cords of headphones and necklaces.

Prickly Pear Drake
Opuntia draco

Common in the southwestern United States including Arizona and
New Mexico, this dragon feeds on Opuntia, also known as paddle
cactus or prickly pear. Oddly, it is able to digest the cacti paddles as
well as the fruit, including cactus spines! 20 inches.

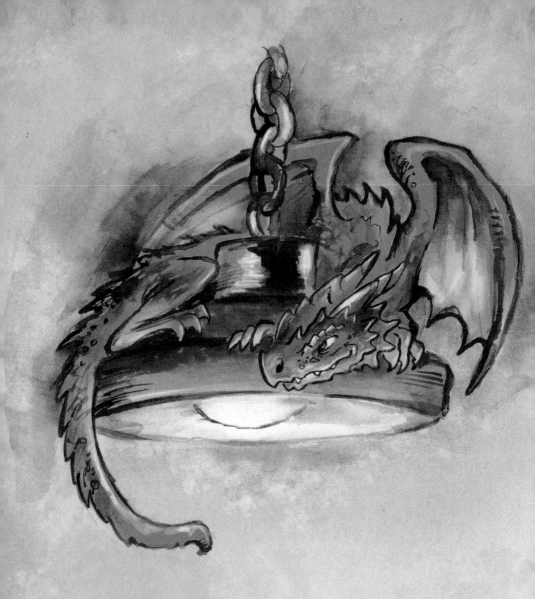

Lamp Lurker
Lucerna umbra draco

This mischievous and stealthy dragon is around 1 to 1.5 feet in length and can be found "lurking" around lamps and on top of light fixtures. The lurker seems drawn to the light bulbs themselves, generally favoring those with softer lighting and enjoys tapping on them when no one is looking. This often causes bulbs to burn out or suddenly blow out with no apparent cause.

Traffic Drake
Vehiculum vigilantes

1-2 feet in size, this dragon is fascinated by traffic and often sits on traffic lights at night to watch the passing cars. While usually unnoticed, it has been known to be the cause of quite a few fender benders if it is agitated. Treat with caution and make no sudden moves around them.

Coca Drake
Draco de scelerisque

Native to South America, Central America, and Mexico, this drake became more common in North America in the 1800's with the growing popularity of chocolate. Feeds on coca leaves and, when domesticated, chocolate bars. When attempting to trap a coca drake one should use chocolate as dark as possible. Measures around 1.7 feet, depending on tail length.

Venomous Drake
Draco venenatorum

This acid spitting drake is 1-2 feet in size and can be identified by its black scales and green eyes. Finding strange objects melted is a sign that you have a venomous drake infestation. Their venom is deadly if not treated within a few hours and is also highly corrosive to any form of metal.

Whisker Drake
Draco scopula pilos

This eastern dragon earned his name from the excessive number of long
whiskers on its face. When alert, these whiskers move at a rapid pace
and provide the dragon with information about its surroundings.
Considered to be a "twitchy" dragon and very difficult to catch. 1.8 feet.

Branch Wyvern
Draco ex ramis

A distant cousin of the larger tree dragon, the branch wyvern is around 1.9
feet and can be spotted coiled around high tree branches. One of the most
widespread dragons, this wyvern feeds mainly on insects and spiders. Can be
domesticated as a form of pest control.

Dairy Drake
Draco de lacticiniis

A lizard-like small (2 feet at most) green dragon only found to inhabit dairies. This odd dragon has a diet of more lactose than most other dragons. Main food sources include milk, cheese and yogurt.

River Serpent
Draco de fluvio

One of the fastest swimming dragons, the small 2 foot river serpent is a joy to watch. Common to small rivers, this dragon is known for its "water dance". This a stunning display of swimming patterns that occurs between males during mating season and resembles a water ballet mixed with a game of chicken. Females will choose the male who appears to be the best swimmer.

Domestic Feather Drake
Domesticis draco plumis

Once common, the feather drake was often smuggled, sold and kept as a domesticated pet. This has endangered the dragon and made them much rarer to encounter. At 2.3 feet, this avian dragon is easily identified by its bright colors and feathered wings. Easy to train. Diet consists of seafood including small fish and shrimp.

Candy Snatcher
Draco rapientem dulcia

This brilliantly colored eastern dragon measures around 2.5 feet and is known for its addiction to sweets. Most often spotted on holidays when candy is most prevalent, the candy snatcher favors brightly colored candy. Very fast moving and fierce.

Seashell Drake
Draco conchis marinis

Common on beaches, the seashell drake collects colorful shells to construct
its sturdy nest. Adults average 2-3 feet in height and can sprint swiftly on
sand using two legs (so that shells can be held at the same time). Often
they make their nests in nearby small caves or nooks in rocks. While they
are not considered aquatic dragons, they can hold their breath for up to
seven minutes.

Lionfish Serpent
Pterois draco

Growing up to 2.8 feet in length, this aquatic dragon resembles lionfish and, while beautiful, has venomous spines. Found in the Indo-Pacific ocean, this sea serpent can best be identified by the brownish banding pattern it bears. Most lionfish serpents live only 7 to 20 years and are usually found in or near coral reefs.

Laundry Lurker
Lauandi insidiator

Bane of laundry mats everywhere, the dreaded laundry lurker is drawn to the smell of detergent and dryer sheets. It loves to nestle itself into a basket of freshly washed clothes for a nice long nap. Between 2 and 3 feet in size, coloration can vary. No relation to the sock snatcher.

Domestic Feline Drake
Domesticis amicus felium

This household dragon is around 2-3 feet and sports muted iridescent colors. This species has an affinity with domestic cats and often enjoys playing with them. For some reason they are hard to spot - possibly due to speed or some type of unknown camouflage. This often results in cats appearing to chase "nothing" around the house. Younger drakes are more green in color and do not display their iridescence until adulthood.

Palm Wyrm
Arecaceae draco

Nests high in palm trees. 2.5 to 3.8 feet. Can be aggressive
when threatened. Diet includes small birds and the fronds of
palm trees. Should be avoided when possible as its bite is
venomous and very deadly.

Lamppost Lurker
Lucerna umbra draco major

These nocturnal dragons are the slightly larger (3-4 feet) relations of the lamp lurker dragon. Most often found in parks or late at night in village streets, the lamppost lurker is drawn to the glow of street lamps and lights and usually curls itself around them. This can cause the lights to flicker or burn out over time. Feeds on mice, bats, and other small rodents.

Rainbow Glider

Lamque humiles draco in caelum

Similar to the sky glider, this wyvern is
easier to spot due to its multi colored
feather wings and plumage. Usually a little
smaller in size (1.8-2.5 feet), this type of
dragon prefers to roost in very tall trees.

Sky Glider
Lamque humiles draco in caelum

Sky gliders are a type of wyvern that is difficult
to spot due to their sky blue backs. While they
have strong wings, they usually prefer to glide
on wind currents. They can grow up to 3 feet
in length and feed mostly on flying insects.
Leathery, bat-like wings. Nests in caves.

Blue Tufted
Wood Wyrm

Red Tufted
Wood Drake

**Yellow Tufted
Wood Drake**

Tufted Wood Dragons
Ligno draco

The tufted wood dragons are known to dwell in remote forests near large trees, often making their nests in the branches or trunk of these trees. Tufted wood drakes are usually 2-3 feet in height, while tufted wood wyrms can grow up to 5 feet in length. There are a number of varieties which are distinguished by the colors of the "tufts" and horns around their faces.

Smog Drake
Fumo Draco

3.7 feet in size, the smog drake is the smaller cousin of the clockwork drake. They appear to feed on smog - drawing in polluted air and breathing out clean air.

Stories say these strange clockwork creatures first appeared during the industrial revolution. Some say they were created by a forward thinking inventor who knew pollution would be an issue someday. Sadly they are rare, making their effect on the environment minimal.

Graveyard Goyle

Draco de sepulcro

Often mistaken for a type of gargoyle, this nocturnal dragon commonly lurks in graveyards. Often poised upon a gravestone or tomb, its stone like coloration and ability to sit still for long periods of time allows it to pass for a statue. Some say the graveyard goyle steals spirits and gnaws the bones of the dead. Others say it guards against grave robbers. Approximately 4.6 feet.

DO NOT
MEDDLE
IN THE
AFFAIRS
OF
DRAGONS

Common Turtle Drake
Draco turturis

Commonly nests near lakes and small ponds in moderate climates. These dragons have osteoderms on their backs that resemble the carapace of many turtles. It is commonly thought that either turtles evolved from these drakes, or these drakes evolved from a type of ancient tortoise. We may never know which came first. Approximately 4.7 feet.

Trashcan Drake
Quisquilias continentis dracone

A scavenger by nature, this dragon has adapted to urban sprawl quite well.
Nocturnal and adept at avoiding discovery by humans. Favors dumpsters
outside Chinese restaurants when available. 4-5 feet in length.

Yellow Brested Wyvern
Parva draco plumis

A little smaller (4-5 feet) than its raindow cousin, this avian feathered dragon mainly inhabits tropical and other warm locals and nests high in trees. Eats a variety of fruits and nuts.

Teal Horned Rope Nibbler

Exterminatore funis

Identified best by its double set of lower, front curving horns, as well as its teal crest. The largest and most heavy duty of the nibbling dragons, the rope nibbler it often found around docks and shipyards, chewing at the rigging of boats. If concerned that one of these may be around, leave a pile of extra rope for it to chew and it will mostly leave functional ropes alone. 6 feet.

Emerald Dragon
Smaragdus draco

The emerald dragon takes its name from his color as well as its preference to nest near formations of emeralds. Common in Egypt, India, and Austria. In ancient times these dragons were sought out for wisdom, especially in matters of the heart. 5 feet from head to tail.

Ruby Dragon
Carbunculus draco

The 5.3 foot ruby dragon is native to the caves of Burma and ice of Greenland, they can be found around large, natural, ruby formations. Rare today, ruby dragons were once thought to be able to cure blood poisoning or other ailments that made people weak. Their beautiful color caused them to be hunted almost to extinction. The location of any remaining ruby dragons is kept secret by dragon watchers.

Flame Dragons
Draco flammarum

An etherial type of dragon between 4 and 8 feet in size, flame dragons appear in or around fire and usually cause the fire to behave erratically. These dragons are the bane of homeowners insurance agents as they cause lots of damage. It is said you can gain much wisdom by gazing into the eyes of a flame dragon, but one should only do so with proper safety precautions (flame retardant clothing etc).

Greater Red Library Drake
Rufus draco de bibliotheca

Able to read multiple books at the same time, this drake devours fiction and non-fiction alike. This dragon is less choosy about its books than the lesser library drake. Most common in rare bookstores and older libraries, the red library drake is mainly nocturnal and is known to leave piles of books in the wrong sections and other such activity that is mistakenly attributed to ghosts. 5-9 feet.

Rock Drake
Draco petram

The rock, or stone drake, measures between 5 and 10 feet. Common in small caves, mountains and other rocky terrain where its hardened outer scales mimic the appearance of rock. This dragon also feeds on rock, retaining their minerals. Perhaps it is this diet that allows a rock dragon to match its domain so well that it is nearly impossible to spot.

Bovine Drake
Vaccam draco

Perhaps one of the strangest species of dragon, the bovine drake takes its name from its strange resemblance to cattle. Unlike cattle, this dragon walks upright (on its back legs) and is probably best identified by its steer like horns. Around 6 feet in size, it feeds on grass and can often be found grazing peacefully among cattle.

Mud Dragon
Draco de lutum

A mid sized (7 foot) dragon, the mud dragon inhabits mud pits, shallow ponds, and muddy cavern pools. Highly carnivorous, it stalks prey while camouflaging both its scales and scent with a thick coating of mud.

Mud dragon diet includes bats, rats, rabbits and other small mammals found in caves and forests.

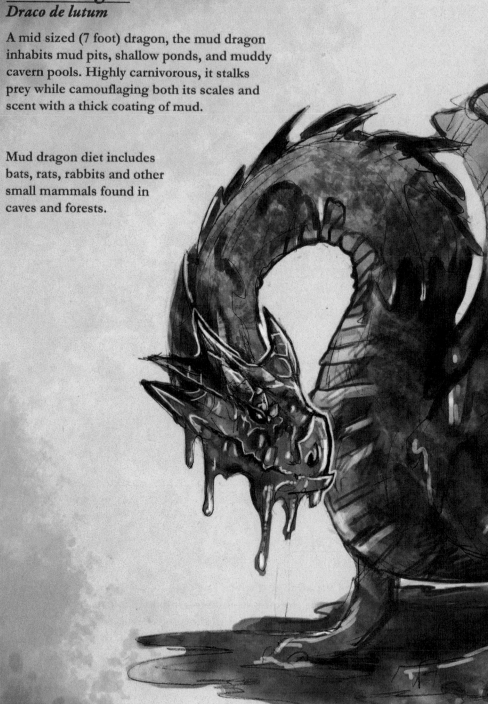

Oak Drake
Quercu petulam dracone

A medium-sized (7 foot) drake with green frilled scales resembling leaves. Found in forests in the Northern Hemisphere, hard to spot as it blends into the foliage easily. Herbivore. Diet includes leaves, seeds and grasses.

Yellow-Breasted Sock Snatcher
Draco soccum abrepta

Uncommon, but widespread, the sock snatcher is very stealthy in spite of its bright coloration and size (8.5 feet). This dragon hoards socks to use as nest lining. The sock snatcher seems to prefer mismatched socks and, if possible, those with bright colors.

Stalactite Wyvren
Draco stalasso petris

Rare to spot, this dragon is nocturnal and sleeps hanging from cave ceilings, usually among a group of stalactites. Like its wingless cousin below, its color allows it to blend in perfectly with the surrounding rock 8 Feet.

Stalagmite Drake
Draco stalagmias petris

Similar in appearance to the stalactite wyvern above, this wingless drake is a little larger (8.5-9 feet) and can be found hiding among stalagmites on cave floors. Also nocturnal, these drakes almost never leave the caves they hatch in.

Banded Feline Dragon
Draconem amicus felium

Larger (8-9 feet) and less domestic than the feline drake, this dragon is known to adopt and care for feral animals, mainly cats. The feline dragon can be best identified by the banded markings on its face, neck and legs as well as its ability to mimic cat sounds.

Arachnid Dragon
Aráneam dracone

This insectoid dragon is thought to be distantly related to
arachnids such as spiders due to the spider-like appendages
along its jawline. Oddly enough the arachnid dragon suffers
from extreme Arachnophobia - a fear
of spiders. Around 11-12 feet tall.

Butterfly Drake
Draco de papilionibus

Dwelling deep in forests, this dragon is likely to be found in areas of high butterfly population. An insectoid dragon, the butterfly drake seems to be attracted to brightly colored butterflies. This dragon is a herbivore and quite tame, but very rare to spot. Measures 12.8 feet in height.

Dormer Drake
Draco de tecto insidens

Around 13 feet in size, this dragon is commonly observed on rooftops where it sometimes appears to be feeding the birds. Most active in early dawn and during sunset.

Jungle Drake
Draconem in truncatis

Rare. Found deep in the darkest of jungles, this 14 foot long dragon was worshiped by native tribes long ago. Now it lives away from human society, ambushing its prey which includes invertebrates, mammals, and small birds. Legends say if you find this mysterious dragon and offer it a garland of bright feathers you will be gifted with long life and good luck.

Ice Drake
Minor draco glácies

At 13.5 feet the ice drake is the smaller cousin of the ice
dragon. Uncommon, makes nests in cold caves and
mountains in Russia and Canada. Often hard to spot due
to its ability to easily blend in with its surroundings. The
ice drake feed mostly on fish and small mammals.

Frost Dragon
Maior draco gelu

The larger cousin of the frost drake, this dragon measures
around 12 feet in length. Just like the smaller drake, the
frost dragon's breath can easily form ice crystals thus creating
"frost". Frost from this dragon can be identified by its spiky
and jagged appearance. Most often spotted during cold snaps
and snow storms.

Snow Drake
Minor draco nix

Often mistaken for a yeti, the snow drake is set apart from other
cold climate dragons by its fur and snub nose. This eastern dragon's
fur allows it to easily blend into snowbanks. Found in snowy
alpine climates, the snow drake measures 9-12 feet.

Rock Wyrm
Petra spiris serpens

Found on remote rock outcroppings and near small caves, the rock wyrm averages 14 feet in length and sports a green/yellow coloring. Females stay in rocky nests while males hunt. Diet consists of mountain dwelling mammals including sheep and goats.

Gate Wyrm
Custos portæ draco

Found on ornate wrought iron gates, this wyrm most often guards
sacred places such as burial grounds, churches, and cemeteries.
Averages 14 feet and is usually a gray green in color.

Great Horned Drake
Draconis magne cornutam

The great horned drake is an avian dragon around 14 feet tall with brown and black markings similar to those of the great horned owl. This drake has a strong kinship with owls, whom often roost in its horns during the day. Like owls, the great horned drake is only active at night, choosing to rest in well hidden spots during the day.

Swamp Dragon

Draco paludem

Uncommon in swamps and marshes, this dragon is very slow moving and
often sleeps for years at a time. Well camouflaged by vegetation, the
swamp dragon is a herbivore and measures around 16 feet. Swamp dragons
are said to be a source of great wisdom and knowledge.

Henge Wyrm
Vetusto saxo draco

This dragon is drawn to forms of Neolithic earthwork, usually the stone circles of the United Kingdom. Measuring around 15 feet in length, the henge wyrm is nocturnal and scarce to spot. Rumors say they somehow dwell underneath the stone circles, but how they access this space is unknown at this time.

Bark Drake
Draco cortice

The bark drake dwells in large forests and woodlands and ranges from 15 to 20 feet in length. They are more likely to be found in older forests, but are hard to spot as their bark-like texture allows them to blend in extremely well. Herbivores, these drakes are known to shelter and protect nearby wildlife. They are generally peaceful, but can be aggressive if they feel their terriorty and its inhabitants are threatened in any way.

Glass Drake
Draco vitro luci

Growing up to 16 feet in length, these dragons acquired their name from their resemblance to glass. Their scales have a strange glass-like transparency, but are actually amazingly strong. Early explorers are said to have used shed scales to start camp fires by focusing sunlight with them, as many today might use a magnifying glass.

Bridge Drake
Sub ponte dracone

Not to be confused with trolls, this drake can be found under bridges as well as underpasses. At 16 feet it is actually quite skittish and moves swiftly. Known for a loud haunting cry (which usually echoes under the bridge) the bridge drake enjoys scaring those who pass by and then vanishes quickly, leaving the witness unsure as to what they saw.

Tree Dragon
Arborem major draconis

Tree dragons average 16.5 feet in length and are the larger cousins of the tree wyvern. They commonly roost on high branches of large trees, but are very difficult to spot. Their scales change color and may be shed depending on the season. This enables the tree dragon to blend into the tree foliage, becoming almost invisible.

Asphalt Wyrm
Bitumen natator

A medium (17.3 feet), gray to orange-brown wyrm with hard, rock-like scales. Commonly found in run down urban areas. The asphalt wyrm lives deep underground, surfacing in early dawn to soak in the first rays of the sun before streets get busy. While rarely seen, the potholes created by these dragons are easily spotted.

Smoke Dragon
Draco de fumo

Made entirely of smoke this dragon is one of the hardest to measure as its size can shift from one moment to the next. Most do not seem to grow much past 18 feet.

Smoke color can vary with black and brown the most common. Smoke dragons can be captured in jars, bottles, lamps and so forth.

Rainbow Wyvern
Magna draco plumis

A bit larger (18.5 feet) than the yellow brested wyvern, this brightly colored, feather dragon mainly inhabits tropical locals. Not territorial, they usually mate for life and live in pairs in secluded jungles. Known to have romping, joyous flights with parrots.

Carriage Drake
Draco qui trahit vehicula

While not as common as they once were, carriage drakes are used to pull small carriages, sleighs, and traps. They are mostly used in secret by affluent explorers as a swift, clean, method of travel. 18-20 feet in size.

Pine Drakes
Pinus dracone major

Red pine drakes are omnivores – feeding on pine nuts and other seeds as well as small rodents and squirrels. They tend to be a bit larger (22 feet) and more aggressive. Green pine drakes are herbivores – choosing to feed only on plants and seeds. They tend to be more docile and a little smaller (19-20 feet). Both varieties favor alpine climates and generally avoid human civilization.

Blue Ridged Bugger
Vehiculo perticam

A mid sized (18 to 30 feet) dragon, buggers have a strange attraction to abandoned cars, usually small ones. They are commonly found in junk yards. The Blue Ridged variety is so named for the blue grass-like spines running the length of its body. This variation has been noted for its fondness of the color red.

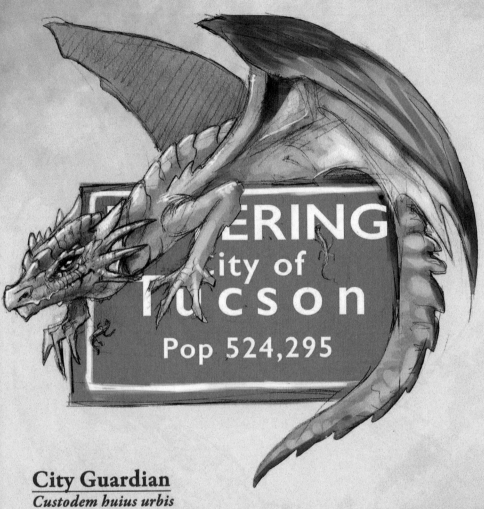

ERING
city of
Tucson
Pop 524,295

City Guardian
Custodem huius urbis

This dragon watches over those that dwell within its domain, usually this is a town or city. Many think of these dragons as the spiritual embodiment of the places they watch over.

Those who love where they live and have settled there for some time seem more likely to spot its guardian than newcomers. Sizes vary depending on the city.

Bengal Hydra
Tigris multa capita draconis

A mid sized (up to 22 feet) hydra this eastern dragon has three to five heads
and is native to India and Nepal. Overall coloration is light orange with some
yellow. May have a white belly. Markings will be black or very dark brown.

Gold Dragon
Vitis draco

One of the better known dragons, the gold dragon averages around 20 feet with a wingspan around 130 feet! These dragons exhibit a territorial guarding behavior and may choose to guard anything from a great treasure to the ruins of an ancient city.

In some cases they may even choose to guard a modern city or building, but will stay out of sight unless a threat to their territory appears.

Sword Serpent
Serpentis maris gladio

Thought to be distantly related to the swordfish, this 18.5 foot aquatic dragon has a long flat sword-like bill which can be used to spear fish. Common in temperate/tropical ocean climates, they swim at a depth of 2200 feet (a bit deeper than swordfish). Can be aggressive. Diet consists of numerous types of fish and small squid.

Ice Dragon
Maior draco glácies

Larger than the frost and ice drakes, the ice dragon is around 21 feet in height. Winters in dark antarctic caves where it may lay clutches of up to ten eggs. Rarely spotted by humans, this dragon often shelters penguins during egg incubation periods.

Clockwork Drake
Draconem in spiritu machina

There is much debate amongst dragon watchers regarding this drake.
Some say it is only a machine and therefore should not count as a dragon.
Others insist that these are dragon spirits that take on physical form using
mechanical parts. The author of this book feels they should be included
and suggests that the reader come to their own conclusions. Clockwork
drakes average around 22 feet in size and are most often found in junk
yards and near factories (probably because parts are easily found there).

African Zebra Drake
Virgatis avis draco

While the zebra drake was named for its resemblance to the zebra, it is actually an avian dragon and shares a kinship with many types of birds. Myths say the zebra drake can actually converse with birds, but it is more likely that it simply enjoys listening to bird song.
Measures 28.7 feet.

Moss Dragon
Draco de silva musco

Around 30 feet, the moss dragon is an ancient forest dragon that can live up to 800 years. They get their name from their symbiotic relationships with plant life including moss, which often grows upon them over time.

Can hibernate for up to 28 years at a time and are very slow moving. Rare and majestic, spotting this dragon is considered a sign of good fortune.

Common Pilot Drake
Draconem amicus gubernatores

Ranging 25 to 32 feet, the pilot drake was commonly used by explorers in the 1800's. By the mid-1900's man made aircraft replaced these drakes and they are now much more rare to spot. There is said to be a secret society of explorers that still travels by drake today, but no proof of this was available at time of this book's publication. Pilot drakes originate from remote mountain ranges and are usually green in color.

Literary Dragon
Magna draco de libris

The largest of the literate dragons, this one grows as large as 30 feet, yet still manages to hoard and read human-sized books. Known to speed read and finish a 300 page novel in under two hours, these rare dragons have great wisdom and are often the secret advisers to kings and presidents.

Stained Glass Dragon
Draco de coloris vitro

A larger cousin to the glass drake, this dragon's scales also have a glass-like appearance but are multicolored. The scales are as hard as bone and can be very sharp, making this pretty dragon quite deadly.

Mostly non-aggressive behavior unless threatened. 32 feet in length. Usually dwells in large caverns.

Clockwork Wyvern
Machinam draco

Now faded mostly into legend, this form of
clockwork dragon was often used for transportation
and dragon watching by early explorers. As noted
with the clockwork dragon, there is much debate as
to if this was simply a machine or also contained a
spirit/life force of its own. Around 25-35 feet, rarely
seen today but a few are still said to exist.

Sunflower Wyrm
Helianthus draco

Named for its resemblance in texture and color to sunflowers, this eastern dragon has layered petal-like yellow scales. Can be found in remote parts of China, usually near farms. Primary eats rice and other grains. 34 feet in length.

Sewer Wyrm
Draco cloacam

This large (35 foot) wyrm has lived in sewer and storm drain systems in major cities since the early 1900's. A carnivore, it feeds mostly on rats and can be very aggressive. Usually nocturnal, avoids daylight. Common in major cities with sewer systems such as New York, Paris, and Moscow.

Shark Drake
Pistrix draco

Growing as large as 40 feet, the shark drake derives its name from its similarities and kinship with sharks. Unlike sharks, this dragon is amphibious, meaning it can dwell on land as well as in water. Can dive as deep as 2000 feet.

Golden Jewelry Hoarder
Accumulator ornamento

This massive (90+ feet) dragon hoards manmade jewelry. Usually living in a deep cave, this gold dragon will have a massive pile of gold and jewels, mostly consisting of necklaces, pendants, crowns and other adornments. It is even known for wearing crowns as rings or bands on its horns. In the past this dragon's diet was mostly on knights and adventurers, but as these have become scarce so too have these dragons.

Ghost Drake
Spiritus draconis

One of the rarest of the dragons is simply known as the ghost drake.
This dragon may be related to the smoke drake, but much less is
known about it. Ghost drakes are reported to fade, flicker, and appear
and disappear in the blink of an eye. A wispy and elusive creature
it is hard to determine their exact size, but most reported sightings
place them between 20 and 30 feet in length.

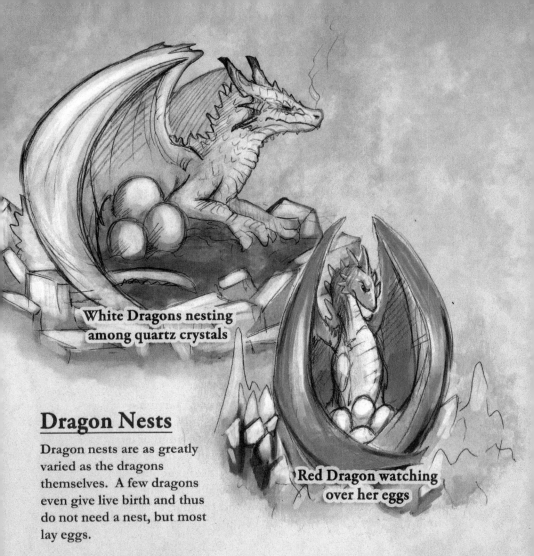

White Dragons nesting among quartz crystals

Red Dragon watching over her eggs

Dragon Nests

Dragon nests are as greatly varied as the dragons themselves. A few dragons even give live birth and thus do not need a nest, but most lay eggs.

These eggs often must be protected for very long incubation periods and sometimes require special treatment. Usually the female dragon will watch over the eggs, or the parents will take shifts over time. In a few varieties the male will watch over the eggs or a group of dragons will take shifts.

The group incubation method is more common for dragons with very long incubation periods as it allows others to hibernate when it isn't their turn to egg-sit. Should you ever come across a dragon's nest it is best to leave it alone as the dragon guarding it may be very defensive and even aggressive in order to protect the eggs.

The Great Hatching

The great hatching takes place deep underground once every 600 to 900 years. Its location is a closely guarded secret passed down from the most dedicated of dragon watchers to their children. This is a time when cave dwelling dragons hatch from massive eggs to repopulate their dwindling numbers. Humans are allowed to observe this amazing process if they are quiet, still, and respectful. Disrespectful watchers are usually fed to the newborn dragons.

Baby Green Dragon
Infantem viride draco

This baby green dragon will grow up to be a large hill dragon, probably at least a half mile in length. As it grows the snout will lengthen as will the duration of its hibernation cycles. In the first ten years of its life it will probably hibernate two or three times for six month periods, but by the time it has reached 50 these will have lengthened to several years of hibernation at a time.

Baby Bronze Dragon
Infantem aeneum draco

A cousin of gold dragons, bronze dragons are usually a little smaller and appear less in myth and legend. This baby is hatching around 30 feet in height, but will only grow to 60 or 70 feet in adult-hood. While it will dwell mostly underground, its scales will acquire more polish and shine with age.

Baby Dragons

The care and feeding of baby dragons is very much species specific, as is the length of time a dragon will remain an infant. In long lived species a dragon might be a baby for hundreds of years, much of which would be spent sleeping or eating. Many baby dragons are able to fend for themselves, having instinctual knowledge of what is safe to eat, where to sleep and so forth. Others may grow up in a community of dragons and be taught how to survive and, of course, how to go unnoticed by humans.

**Rare
Fire/Ice
Hybrid**

**Rare
Water/Rock
Hybrid**

Hybrid Dragons

Many dragon species can, and do, cross-breed. Usually this occurs between those that are similar in size, type and habitat such as a bark dragon breeding with a swamp dragon. Rare cases of unusual hybrids exist, but they are usually singular in nature.

Lightning Wyvern
Draco fulminis

The large 15 yard lightning wyvern is only visible during flashes of lighting. High flying, this dragon is often little more than a shadow in the sky, but seems to feed upon the electrostatic discharge of lightning during storms. More common in tropical locations.

Sand Wyvern
Harena turbine draconis

Measuring 58 feet in length (about 19 yards), the sand wyvern inhabits large, rocky desert environments. These dragons are often responsible for causing sandstorms, especially during mating season when females may compete for the attention of a male.

Skin has a rocky, worn texture and females are generally a little smaller than the males.

60 FEET

Ridged Pachyderm Snatcher
Rapientem elephanti

This large (25-30 yard) dragon is known for snatching pachyderms such as rhinos, elephants, and hippos. In spite of their bright coloration and massive size, this type of snatcher is rare and hard to spot.

Stories say...

Early legends refer to "Elephantis orator" (the elephant speaker) and claim these dragons could converse with pachyderms.

Yet other legends call them "Devoratrix elephanti" (devourer of elephants) and say they've caused many elephant deaths that were later blamed on poaching.

12 FEET

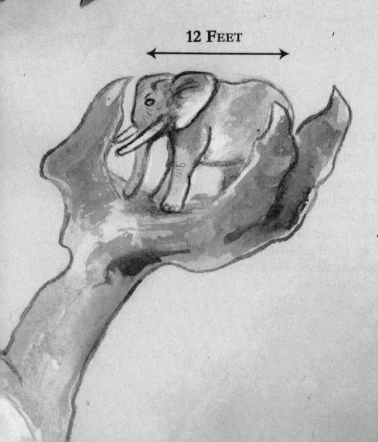

Lake Serpent
Serpens ex lacu

Legends of lake "monsters" are often due to this surprisingly gentle aquatic dragon. The lake serpent has a lifespan of up to 625 years and has been captured in a number of blurry photos which are often called hoaxes. Patient children willing to keep them secret are often gifted with the friendship of these amazing dragons. Around 60 feet in length

Yellow Breasted Sun Drake

Draco solis

This large (62 foot) dragon is still considered small by comparison with
the sunrise and sunset draconis. Inhabits mountain ranges and can be
observed absorbing sunshine high on clifftops.

Cavern Drake
Draco cavernae minor

Smaller than the cavern dragon, this drake grows between
18-26 yards and generally nests deep in caverns, favoring
those with moderately warm climates and water supplies.
They live hundreds of miles underground so only the most
dedicated spelunking dragon watchers can find them.

Moon Dragon
Draco chorus lunæ

An eastern dragon, this large 30 yard (90 feet) dragon is only seen on the
full moon. The moon dragon is seen to fly in slow, intricate patterns,
basking in the moonlight. Often accompanied by large flocks of bats.
It is unclear where this dragon goes when the moon is not full, or if,
perhaps, we simply cannot see it the rest of the time.

Lava Drake
Solumque est draco

Most common near volcanic activity or hot springs.
35-40 yards in size, the smaller cousin of the lava lord.
Eggs must be kept hot (100 degree fahrenheit minimum)
for over sixty years before hatching. Grouchy when first
awoken, but generally even tempered the rest of the
time.

Shale Draconis
Acuto petram dracone

This massive (30-80 yard) dragon lives in remote mountain ranges and is one of the larger rock dragons. Like most rock dragons it has the ability to blend in perfectly with other rocks and go unnoticed. Usually solitary except during mating seasons. Shale dragon eggs must be kept warm and guarded for hundreds of years before they hatch.

Clocktower Dragon
Horologium turris dracone

A much larger (up to 80 yards in size) relative of the common clock drake, this dragon is drawn to large clocks – usually those in clocktowers. Dragon watchers have theorized that it is the repetitive sounds made by the clocks that draw these dragons. Can be highly territorial about a given clocktower.

Sea serpent
Serpentis Maris

Perhaps the best known of the aquatic dragons, the sea serpent is between 38-85 yards long. It suffers from an irresistible urge to destroy anything on the surface of its territory. This has made it legendary for destroying boats, ships, ocean liners and even the occasional submarine. Most commonly found in Bermuda and parts of the Caribbean.

Deep Sea Hydra
Profúndum maris dracone

This massive (up to 100 yards!) aquatic dragon dwells in the deep sea - the lowest layer of ocean that is below 13000 feet. Extremely rare and spotted by only the most diligent underwater explorers, the deep sea hydra does not like to be disturbed. Many sea monster legends are said to originate with this dragon.

Hill Drake
Colle magna draco

Hill drakes hibernate from anywhere between 50 and 90 years at a time, with life spans over 1000 years. As part of their hibernation processes they burrow into the ground, causing a thick layer of soil to settle over their scales. Over time plants and trees take root in this soil, growing up to camouflage the dragon even further. Rare and almost impossible to spot. 15-28 Yards in size.

Island Dragon
Insulam dracone

Similar to the cavern dragon, the island dragon sleeps for extended periods and can be very large (well over 100 yards). Plant and wildlife often can make a home on this floating aquatic dragon while it sleeps, leading it to be mistaken for a small island.

Deep Sea Sneel
Profúndum maris cetus draco

The sneel is a massive (140 yard) aquatic dragon with whale like flippers.
Feeds on sea life including smaller whales, shellfish, and even squid. Unlike
most dragons, sneels have live birth (like mammals) instead of laying eggs.
Most common in the North Pacific ocean, these dragons come closer to the
surface to feed at night, but sleep in deep underwater caves during the day.

Gold Scaled Draconis
Aurum draco immani

Much larger than the traditional gold dragon and rare to find. Makes its habitat in remote wilderness areas. While it usually does have a cave based lair, this massive (162 yard) dragon often ventures out to feed on trees. Herbivore and mostly harmless (unless one steps on you by mistake).

Cloud Drake
Nubibus draconis

This large (170 yard) wingless eastern dragon can be spotted on clear days high among the clouds. Known for its joyous flight patterns and whimsical vapor trails. Feeds mainly on trees and shrubs.

Lava Lord
Draco ardentis solumque

A massive (1-2 miles in size!) subterranean dragon, the lava lord
dwells deep underground, usually in the vicinity of a volcano. Males
tend to have brighter colors than females. Usually solitary except
during mating seasons which occur every 500-800 years and can result
in volcanic activity.

Cavern Dragon
Draco cavernae major

Rare and known to sleep for up to four hundred years at a
time, these dragons often go unnoticed simply because they
are so large (200-300 Yards). Their rock-like exterior allows
them to blend in so perfectly that people pass them by. It is
said that earthquakes are a sign that a cavern drake is
waking up from its nap, but this has not yet been proven.

Iceberg Draconis
Insulam glácies draco

Often camouflaged in plain sight, these aquatic dragons tend to float, or drift, partly above water like icebergs. Can grow as large as 3 miles in size! Often have long, deep, hibernation cycles. Most common near glaciers. Rumor has it that a famous ocean liner once crashed into an iceberg draconis, but no proof of this has ever been discovered.

Asteroid Drake
Asteroidem dracone

This giant, four mile high dragon likes to "piggy back" rides through space on asteroids, only flying short distances itself. It would appear these dragons have a way to tell the path and speed of a given asteroid, but how they do this is currently a mystery. Can be spotted only with the most powerful of telescopes and, of course, if you happen to be looking at the right asteroid.

Comet Dragon
Draco cometa

Often mistaken for a shooting star,
this 7 mile long dragon travels around
the galaxy at a rapid pace.

Believed to be some type of fire
elemental, the comet dragon
leaves a bright tail of fire in
its wake.

Crater Wyrm
Luna crateris draco

These huge lunar dragons can grow as large as 8 miles and usually nest in
craters. They are able to blend in with the surface of the moon which makes
them hard to see from earth, even with a good telescope. A few astronauts
have been lucky enough to observe them and, finding them to be gentle
creatures, they have mostly kept them secret from the general public. It is
thought that these dragons feed on minerals found in moon rocks.

Star Wyvern
Draco stellarum

Growing up to 12 Miles, the ancient star wyvern is a rare astral dragon.
Like many smaller guardian dragons, this wyvern usually chooses to
watch over a specific star, never straying far from it. Legends say that
the light of the chosen star nourishes the dragon and when the star
goes out the wyvern will too. Since most stars are over a billion years
old, this may make star wyverns the oldest of dragons.

Red-Ridged Planet Hoarder
Planeta draconis abrepta

Planet hoarders are some of the largest dragons - measuring 4200-5000 Miles
in size! Each hoarder "nest" is usually an entire galaxy containing countless
hoarded planets collected over millions of years. Most planet hoarders are
slow and rarelyvisible or detectable by the inhabitants of the planets they
collect. They peacefully coexist with other species of astronomical dragon.

Sunrise & Sunset Draconis
Solis draco

Spotted at sunrise and sunset, these astrological dragons are massive –
ranging from 5000 to 8000 miles in length. They flow in slow circling
patterns around the sun and are rarely spotted due to the sun's glare.

Galaxy Draconis
Draco de galaxiae

The largest known dragon is simply deemed "astronomical" in size. Little is known about the galaxy draconis, save what is mentioned in a few journals and legends. It is said to travel between galaxies and be so old as to have witnessed the creation of the universe itself.

Index by Type

Amphibious

Aquatic

Avian

Baby

Clockwork

Gremlin

Hydra

Insectoid

Literary

Rock

Wyrm

Wyvern

Index by Name

About the Author

Jessica Cathryn Feinberg is an artist, writer, and
creative warrior living in Tucson, Arizona with four crazy
cats and one very chill dog.

When she isn't busy with her creative work, she can be
found feeding her bibliophilia, walking her dog, and
having adventures with the local dragons and fae.

Jessica can be found at many of southwest
comic and fantasy conventions too!

Check out more art and Jessica's event schedule online at:
http://www.artlair.com